W9-DAA-324

Blaze and the Mountain Lion

by C. W. Anderson

MACMILLAN PUBLISHING CO., INC.
New York
COLLIER MACMILLAN PUBLISHERS
London

© C. W. Anderson 1959

All rights reserved. No part of this book may be reproduced or utilized in any form or by any means, electronic or mechanical, including photocopying, recording or by any information storage and retrieval system, without permission in writing from the Publisher.

Library of Congress catalog card number: 59-11293

ISBN 0-02-702630-2

Macmillan Publishing Co., Inc.

866 Third Avenue, New York, New York 10022

Collier Macmillan Canada, Inc.

Printed in the United States of America

20   19   18   17   16   15   14   13

To Cyrus

Billy was a boy who had a pony named Blaze that he loved very much. His parents had come west and taken a ranch house for the summer and they brought Blaze along, too. Billy and Blaze loved the west and went for long rides every day.

They loved to explore the wide open country. There was so much to see. They knew the old badger who had his hole nearby and liked to sit in the sun. Sometimes they saw a coyote disappearing like a gray shadow in the brush.

Billy had an old rope that he used as a lasso.
Jim, his cowboy friend, had showed him how to
throw it. As he rode along, he practiced catching
bushes and sage brush. Blaze always stopped when
he saw the rope fly through the air, just like a
trained cow pony.

One day Billy started off very early for the distant hills. It was his favorite place to explore. He was sure that many animals lived in that wild place.

Soon he saw a large herd of cattle in the distance and a cowboy was with them. Billy knew it was his friend Jim and he waved to him.

Jim was glad to see him. When he told Jim where he was going Jim said, "Look out for that big mountain lion that has been killing our calves."

"Would he attack Blaze and me?" asked Billy frightened.

"No, a mountain lion is afraid of man. He would never attack you, but he's tough on calves. There is a big bounty on this fellow, but he's smart. No one ever gets a shot at him and we can't find where he lives."

As Billy rode along he thought about the mountain lion. That this fierce creature should kill helpless calves seemed very cruel. He hoped he would see him and perhaps find out where he lived.

As they were climbing the hills Billy pulled Blaze to a halt. There in a place where the earth was soft was a big track. It looked like a dog's track but it was very much bigger than even the biggest dog would make. Billy felt a shiver run down his back. The mountain lion had been here!

Now Billy was watching everything very care-fully. He noticed that Blaze was snorting and seemed very nervous. Then Billy saw part of the skeleton of a calf behind a bush. Now he knew they were near where the mountain lion lived!

Then Billy saw him! He was crouched as if ready to spring. Billy had never realized how big and fierce a mountain lion could be. If he had not remembered that Jim said they were afraid of people, Billy would have been very frightened.

Just then the animal caught sight of them. With a few big bounds he disappeared into a large dark hole.

"That's his cave," cried Billy. "Wait till I tell Jim!"

When they reached the very top of the ridge and looked down, Billy saw why the mountain lion was there. A little calf was standing on a narrow ledge below. He had slipped over the edge trying to get away from the mountain lion. The rock was so steep he could not get back up. Far below were sharp rocks.

Billy uncoiled the old rope he used as a lasso, then lay down on the ledge and waited. The little calf was calling for its mother and was moving around very frightened.

Just then the little calf reared up. Billy threw his lasso and the loop went around the little calf's body. Billy quickly pulled it snug. Now he felt he could save the helpless calf. He had a plan.

Billy quickly tied the end of his rope to the saddle horn. "We can save this little calf," Billy said to Blaze. "Just be slow and careful."

Blaze seemed to understand, for when Billy led him away he went very quietly. Billy only hoped the old rope would hold. When he saw the little calf safely on top he was very happy. "That was fine," he said as he patted Blaze.

Billy patted the little calf and talked quietly to him. Then he took off the lasso and tied the rope around the calf's neck. He did not want to leave him so near the mountain lion and he was sure he belonged to Jim's herd.

The little calf walked along quietly beside Blaze. He seemed to know he was now with friends and safe from the fierce mountain lion.

"Good boy!" said Jim when he heard Billy's story. "I'm proud of both of you. Now that I know where that fellow lives I'll get him. Just wait and see."

As they jogged along toward home, Billy felt very gay and happy.

"You are a fine pony," he said to Blaze. "Jim said so and he knows. He's proud of you and so am I."

A few days later when Billy again saw Jim he came toward them with a wide smile.

"I got the mountain lion," he said. "There was a big bounty on him and with part of it I bought you this." It was the most beautiful lasso Billy had ever seen. When he thanked Jim for it Jim said, "You earned it. If it weren't for you, that mountain lion would still be killing our calves."

How beautifully the new lasso sailed through the air. Now Billy felt he could never miss. Maybe someday he would be a fine roper like Jim. Billy was very happy and Blaze went along so gaily that Billy knew he was happy, too.

By C. W. Anderson

Billy and Blaze
Blaze and the Gypsies
Blaze and the Forest Fire
Blaze Finds the Trail
Blaze and Thunderbolt
Blaze and the Mountain Lion
Blaze and the Indian Cave
Blaze and the Lost Quarry